POKÉMON®

Time Out for Torchic

Adapted by
Tracey West and
Katherine Noll

OFFICIAL
Pokémon®
MASTER'S
CLUB

SCHOLASTIC INC.
New York   Toronto   London   Auckland   Sydney
Mexico City   New Delhi   Hong Kong   Buenos Aires

Published by Scholastic Inc.
90 Old Sherman Turnpike, Danbury, CT 06816.

SCHOLASTIC and associated logos are trademarks and/or registered trademarks of
Scholastic Inc.

ISBN 0-439-72096-6

First Scholastic Printing, October 2004

Ash, Pikachu, and May were on their way to a new town.

"Let's race!" Ash said. "I can't wait for our next adventure!"

"Slow down," May said. "First, I need to learn more about my Pokémon."

"Use your Pokédex," Ash said.

May took out her small electronic gadget. She looked up the name of her Pokémon, Torchic.

"It says that Torchic is a Fire Pokémon," May said. "It has many attacks . . ."

9

Just then a Pokémon crossed their path.

"Look!" Ash cried. "There is an Azurill!"

"It is so cute," May said. "I want to catch it!"

May threw a Poké Ball at Azurill.

The Poké Ball hit Azurill.
Azurill popped in.
But Azurill popped right back out!
"First you have to battle Azurill,"
Ash told May. "*Then* you can throw
a Poké Ball at it."

"Right," May said. "Torchic, I choose you!"

Torchic came out of its Poké Ball.

"Use Peck attack, Torchic!" May cried.

Torchic ran at Azurill. But it missed!
Torchic's beak got stuck in a tree.

Torchic tried again. It hit Azurill with a flame attack.

But Azurill was not alone. Torchic ran right into Azumarill and Marill, too!

The three Pokémon blasted
Torchic.
Torchic fainted!

"We need to get Torchic to a Pokémon Center," Ash said.

The friends ran as fast as they could. On the way, they came to a strange place. Tall rocks rose up from the ground.

A man was looking at the rocks.
His name was Professor Aldon.
He told Ash and May how to get to
the Pokémon Center.

They soon reached the Pokémon Center. May ran up to Nurse Joy. "Can you please help my Torchic?" May asked.

Nurse Joy hooked up Torchic's Poké Ball to a machine.

"Torchic is fine," she said. "It just needs a good night's sleep."

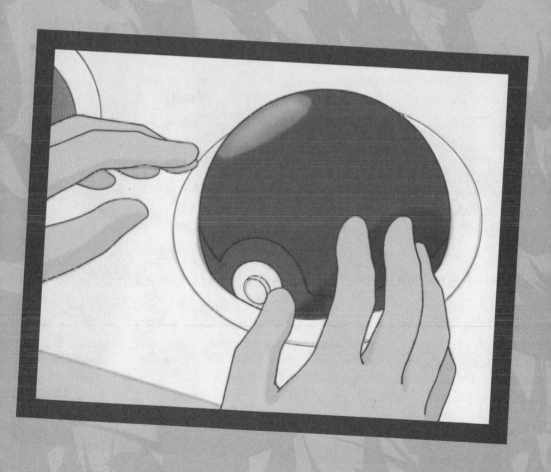

Ash, May, and Pikachu walked around the Pokémon Center.

They ran into Professor Aldon again! He told them all about the strange city of rocks.

"There is a stone room there," he said. "Legend says that it links our world to the ancient Pokémon world."

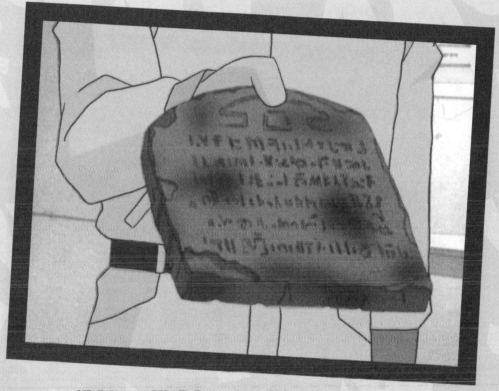

"Wow!" May said.

"This tablet tells how to enter the room," said the professor. "But," he added, "four keys are needed to open the door."

Then the lights went out!
Some people ran in. Three
Houndoom growled at their feet.
It was Team Magma!

Nurse Joy ran into the room.
"There is no power in the Pokémon
Center," she shouted.

Suddenly Team Magma grabbed Professor Aldon. "Take us to the city of rocks," said their leader to the professor.

Team Magma locked Ash and the others in a storeroom.
Then they took away the professor.

"Oh no!" cried Nurse Joy. "We must turn on the power. The Pokémon being healed are in danger!"

"*Pika pika!*" said Pikachu. The little Pokémon found a way out— through the air shafts!

Ash, May, and Pikachu crawled through the air shafts.

They found their way to the main desk. They turned on the power.

"Good job!" Ash said. "Now we have to help Professor Aldon."

Team Magma forced Professor Aldon to lead them to the rock city.

"We have the four keys," their leader said. "Tell us how to open the door. We want to get to the ancient Pokémon world."

Professor Aldon placed each key in a special place on the door.

The door opened! The walls inside the room were carved with drawings. But there were no Pokémon.

"These pictures show people and ancient Pokémon living together," said the professor. "Amazing!"

"Who cares about drawings?" snapped the leader of Team Magma. "We want to capture some ancient Pokémon."

Team Magma left in a helicopter.
Ash, May, and Pikachu ran up to
the professor.
"Are you okay?" asked Ash.
"I am fine," said Professor Aldon.

But everything was not fine. Ash heard a noise by the door.

It was Team Rocket!

"We'll just take these keys," said Meowth.

"Pikachu! Stop them!" Ash cried.

Jessie sent out Arbok to battle
Pikachu.

Pikachu slammed Arbok with
Quick Attack.

Arbok slammed into Team Rocket.
Then Pikachu zapped them all
with Thundershock.

"Looks like we are blasting off
again!" Team Rocket cried.

The keys rolled back to Professor
Aldon. He put them back in the door.
Then something amazing
happened. The sun rose in the sky.
When the sun's rays hit the keys,
the room began to move. The stone
floor slid open!

The four friends walked down
the stairs. They came to a big cave
and a lake.

33

Something moved in the water.
A Pokémon jumped out of the lake.

"It is the ancient Pokémon Relicanth!" cried Professor Aldon.

"Then it is true," said Professor Aldon. "This room is a link to the ancient Pokémon world."

"It's a good thing Team Magma did not find it," said Ash.

The friends went back to the Pokémon Center. May picked up her Torchic. It was all better.

"Let's race to the next town, Ash," May said. "I can't wait to have another Pokémon adventure!"

Pokémon TRIVIA

Who's That Fire Pokémon?

37

See page 45 for the answer.

A Test of Tails

Can you tell who these Fire Pokémon are by just looking at their tails?

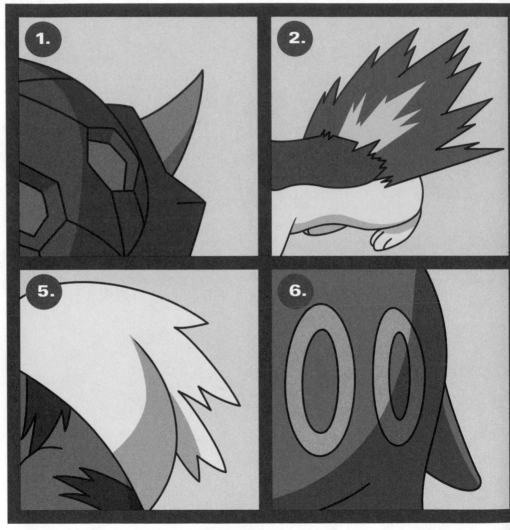

Check page 45
or your *Fire Pokédex*
for the answers.

Battle Time!

Now it is your turn to battle! Read about each battle below. Then pick the best Pokémon to use against your opponent. In each battle, all of the Pokémon are the same level.

1. The battle starts. Your opponent throws out a Poké Ball. Out pops a cute Fire Pokémon—a Torchic! Which Pokémon has the best chance of beating it?

Treecko™
(Grass)

Mudkip™
(Water)

Wurmple™
(Bug)

2. *"Pika! Pika!"* Your opponent has chosen a Pikachu. Which of these Pokémon will do best against this Electric Pokémon?

Corphish™
(Water)

Taillow™
(Normal/Flying)

Phanpy™
(Ground)

3. Here comes Bayleef, a Grass Pokémon. Pick a Pokémon to battle against Bayleef.

Combusken™
(Fire/Fighting)

Marshtomp™
(Water/Ground)

Skitty™
(Normal)

41

Check page 45 or your *Fire Pokédex* for the answers.

Which Pokémon Doesn't Belong?

Look at the three Pokémon in each row.
Two Pokémon are related by Evolution.
Can you guess which one is *not* related?

1. Torchic™   Taillow™   Blaziken™

2. Camerupt™   Numel™   Miltank™

3. Treecko™   Cyndaquil™   Typhlosion™

4.

Houndour™ **Houndoom™** **Mightyena™**

5.

Slugma™ **Diglett™** **Magcargo™**

6.

Ho-Oh™ **Charmander™** **Charmeleon™**

7.

Arcanine™ **Poochyena™** **Growlithe™**

43

Check page 45
or your *Fire Pokédex*
for the answers.

Fire Pokémon Jokes

Why did Slugma pour hot chocolate on itself?

To cool off!

What do you get when you cross a Charizard and a cheese sandwich?

A grilled cheese sandwich!

What do you give an angry Typhlosion for its birthday?

Anything it wants!

Why did Ash look for the Torkoal on the ceiling?

Because he heard that heat rises!

What do you do if your Fire Pokémon is having a heat wave?

You wave back!

Why didn't Mrs. Ketchum want Ash to catch a Charmander?

Because she didn't want him playing with fire!

Answers

Page 37: Who's That Fire Pokémon? Ninetales!

Pages 38-39: A Test of Tails
1. Torkoal
2. Quilava
3. Ninetales
4. Vulpix
5. Growlithe
6. Camerupt
7. Magmar
8. Ponyta

Pages 40-41: Battle Time!
1. Mudkip (Water beats Fire)
2. Phanpy (Ground beats Electric)
3. Combusken (Fire beats Grass)

Pages 42-43: Which Pokémon Doesn't Belong?
1. Taillow
2. Miltank
3. Treecko
4. Mightyena
5. Diglett
6. Ho-Oh
7. Poochyena